I Don't Like GLORIA!

For Alfie and Charlie – K. U.

For Ruth, Lowell and Cara,
with love – M. C.

First published 2007 by Walker Books Ltd
87 Vauxhall Walk, London SE11 5HJ

This edition published 2008

10 9 8 7 6 5 4 3 2

Text © 2007 Kaye Umansky
Illustrations © 2007 Margaret Chamberlain

The right of Kaye Umansky and Margaret Chamberlain to be identified as
author and illustrator respectively of this work has been asserted by them in
accordance with the Copyright, Designs and Patents Act 1988

This book has been typeset in Gill Sans.

Printed in Singapore

British Library Cataloguing in Publication Data: a catalogue record for this
book is available from the British Library

ISBN: 978-1-4063-1340-6

www.walkerbooks.co.uk

I Don't Like GLORIA!

words by **Kaye Umansky**   pictures by **Margaret Chamberlain**

WALKER BOOKS
AND SUBSIDIARIES

LONDON • BOSTON • SYDNEY • AUCKLAND

I don't like Gloria.

She's a cat.

She's come to live with us.

Nobody asked me.

The first thing she did
was go and eat from
my dish.

MY dish.

GLORIA COLIN

She's got her own dish.
It says GLORIA on it.
Mine says COLIN.

Can't she read?

I growled at her
and got told off.

Is that fair?

I don't like

Gloria.

Gloria has taken over the house!
She even sleeps in my basket.

On my special cushion.

They forgot my walk yesterday.

Too busy fussing over Gloria.

She's taken over the garden now!
MY garden. I tried chasing her
up a tree. She wouldn't run.

I felt silly.

They told me off for barking at her.

Can you believe it?

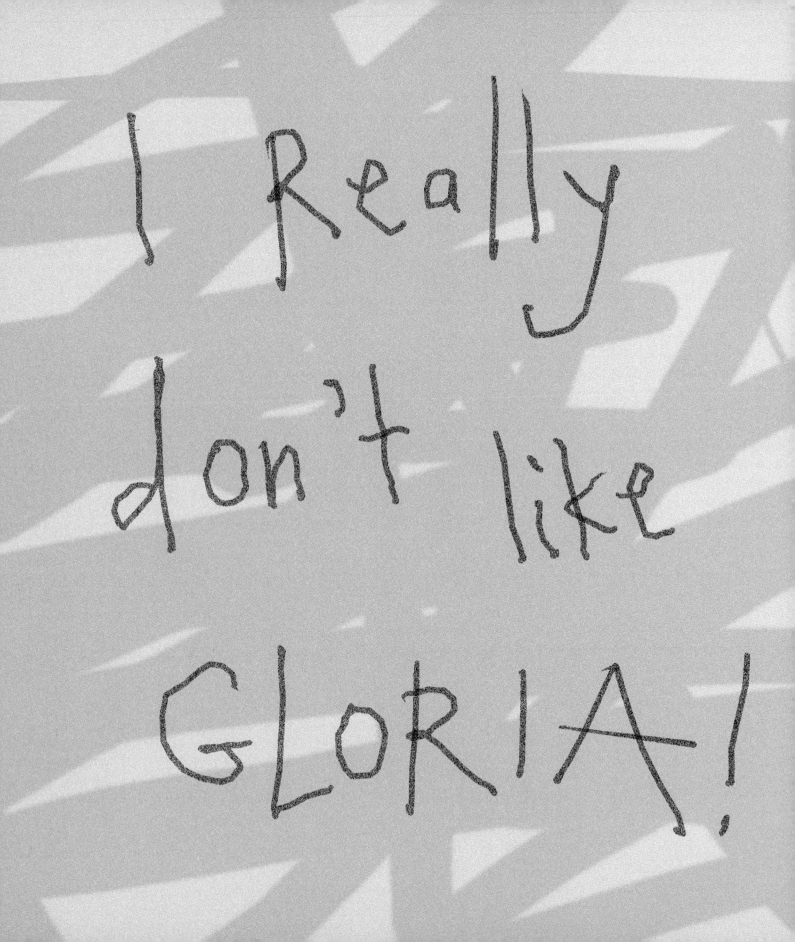

But hey, what's this?!
A big cardboard box
has arrived.

THIS
WAY
UP

I go to investigate.
They push me back.
Gloria goes to investigate.
They push her back too!

But we saw.
We saw all right.

His name is Jeffrey. He's a rabbit.
He's come to live with us.

Now nobody's taking any
notice of me and Gloria.

Too busy fussing
over Jeffrey.

I still don't like Gloria
and Gloria doesn't like me.

But at least we agree
on one thing.

We REALLY
don't like Jeffrey!